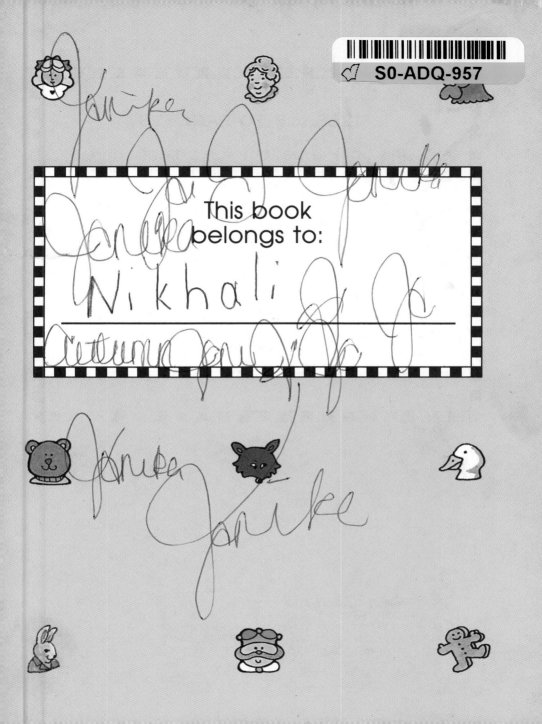

This book
belongs to:

Nikhali

MESSAGE TO PARENTS

This book is perfect for parents and children to read aloud together. First read the story to your child. When you read it again run your finger under each line, stopping at each picture for your child to "read." Help your child to figure out the picture. If your child makes a mistake, be encouraging as you say the right word. Point out the written word beneath each picture in the margin on the page. Soon your child will be "reading" aloud with you, and at the same time learning the symbols that stand for words.

Copyright © 1988 Checkerboard Press, Inc. All rights reserved.
READ ALONG WITH ME books are conceived by Deborah Shine.
READ ALONG WITH ME and its logo are trademarks of Checkerboard Press, Inc.
Library of Congress Catalog Card Number: 88-25718 ISBN: 002-898131-6
Printed in the United States of America 0 9 8 7 6 5 4 3

Checkerboard Press, Inc.
30 Vesey Street, New York, New York 10007

The Story of Peter Rabbit

A Read Along With Me Book

Retold by Joan Powers

Illustrated by Kitty Diamantis

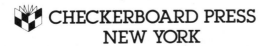
CHECKERBOARD PRESS
NEW YORK

four

Peter

Mother

house

tree

Once upon a time there were

 little rabbits named Flopsy,

Mopsy, Cottontail, and .

They all lived with their in a

small beneath a large .

"Now, my dears," said their
one day, "you may go out and
play in the fields or pick in
the lane. But stay away from
Mr. McGregor and his .
You know what happened to
your father there. Mrs. McGregor
put him in a ."

berries

garden

pie

Mother

bonnet

umbrella

store

buns

 took her and her

 and went off to the to

buy some  .

Flopsy, Mopsy, and Cottontail were good little and went off to pick down by the lane.

But , who was very, very naughty, ran to Mr. McGregor's and quickly squeezed under the .

rabbits

berries

Peter

garden

gate

Peter

lettuce

green beans

carrot

parsley

cucumbers

First,  ate some and some . Then he ate some . By now had begun to feel a little sick, so he looked around for some . But as he came near the , he saw Mr. McGregor.

"Stop!" cried Mr. McGregor. He grabbed a and chased after .

 was very frightened. He ran all around the looking for the . He lost one among the and the other one among the .

rake

garden

gate

slipper

cabbages

potatoes

Peter

jacket

fence

In his haste did not look where he was going, and his got caught on a 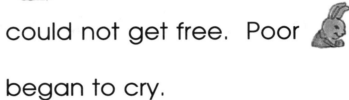. pulled and pulled but he could not get free. Poor began to cry.

But just then a flock of

came along and urged him to try

harder to get free. Finally

struggled out of his  and ran

off. Mr. McGregor was right

behind him. ran into the

 and hid inside a watering

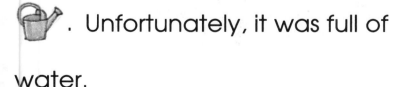 . Unfortunately, it was full of

water.

birds

shed

can

Peter

shed

rake

Mr. McGregor was sure that  was hiding in the 🏠 and began to look for him. Suddenly 🐰 sneezed — a very, very loud *kerchoo!* — and Mr. McGregor picked up his 🔧 and was after him again. 🐰 upset some

as he jumped out the .

Mr. McGregor was tired of

chasing , so he went back to

raking his garden.

plants

window

Peter

garden

house

 wandered slowly around

tree

the . He just had to get

back to his small beneath

the large .

mouse

He saw a and asked her

the way out of the garden, but

she had some large in her

mouth and couldn't answer.

 started to cry again. He

came to a . A white

was sitting and watching a .

 didn't ask her the way. He

knew no would help him, so

he walked by.

peas

pond

cat

fish

Peter

bush

Then heard a scraping

noise, so he hid under a .

After a while climbed

onto a wheelbarrow to see

what was making the sound. It

was Mr. McGregor working with

his  . And just beyond him

was the ! hopped

down and ran as fast as he

could to the . He ran out

the and all the way home

to his under the big .

hoe

gate

house

tree

Peter

house

bed

Mother

jacket

slippers

When reached his

he flopped down on his nice soft

 and closed his eyes.

wondered what had become

of his and .

did not feel very well that evening. made him some camomile tea for supper while Flopsy, Mopsy, and Cottontail had delicious  and and .

And what did happened to 's and ? Why, Mr. McGregor made a with them to frighten away the .

buns

berries

milk

scarecrow

birds